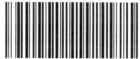

Actually, I Can

(AND SO CAN YOU!)

DOLLY HARDY

Special Thanks...

A very special thank you to
Dianna Hemmingway
for her illustrations,
her kind and generous heart, and her
overall positivity.

"The power you have is
to be the best version
of yourself you can be,
so you can create a
better world."

Ashley Rickards

Introduction

Okay, if you're reading this, it's because someone thinks you're pretty awesome. Someone thinks you deserve to become part of this amazing sisterhood of strong, powerful and overall super cool & totally fabulous girls.

So, here's what you need to do. Right now. Stop reading. Go find the person who gave you this book. Did a librarian pick it out for you? Your mom, sister or bff?

Did someone send it in the mail to you? Well, whatever way you got it, no matter how you got it, I want you to stop and thank that person, because what you're about to read will stay with you for the rest of your life.

And hey, if you found this book on your own? Well, that is just super awesome! Good for you!

So, before we begin, let me just tell you something; I'm not famous. Believe it or not, I don't have an Instagram account with over 100,000 followers. I don't have a Snapchat account or TikTok following.

And you know what? You don't need to be famous or try to be *like* someone famous to be totally awesome.

We are all different. Some of us are tall, some are not so tall. Some of us are blonde, brunette, or redheads. We are rockin' our purple and blue hair, even!

We are gymnast girls, soccer chicks & hockey beasts! We are talent-show singers, lunchroom lovers, and recess renegades!

We are killin' it on Fortnite, building worlds on Minecraft, and creating videos on YouTube.

We are all different, and we are all amazing.

So, while I'm not famous like Taylor Swift, JoJo Siwa, or any of those fantastic TikTok teens, I do believe that everyone has a voice. Everyone has a story. Some have yet to be written, while others are creating theirs as they go along.

This book is kind of a mix between some of my stories, and a guide for getting through some of the challenges you're facing, or will face, as you get a bit older.

My hope for you, is that after you read this, you feel empowered, you feel validated, and maybe even a little relieved that you're not the only one going through this stuff.

And hey, wanna hear something cool? All the illustrations in this book were done by a 14-year old girl who's totally killin' it with her art!

Her name is Dianna Hemmingway. And when I asked her to sketch out some ideas for the book, I thought her rough sketches were so perfect, so raw, I wanted to use them instead of the clean & crisp final drawings she created.

Listen, you'll want to remember her name, because she just might be the next Monet or Van Gogh or Picasso.

"The great thing about
new friends is that they
bring new energy to
your soul."

Shanna Rodriguez

Dedication

This goes out to my childhood friends. To Lisa, Christine, Diane, Linda, and MaryBeth. I would never have survived my pre-teen years without you.

To my husband Shawn, who never waivers in his support of me, his love and commitment to me and our children, and the only one who truly gets my level of crazy. You have my heart.

To my children, John, Patrick, and Lila - thank you for blessing me with the greatest role of all, the role of being your mom.

"When life knocks you down, you can choose whether or not to get back up."

Karate Kid

Table of Contents

Before We Begin

I've been thinking about how insane things feel right now. It seems you can't say anything, do anything or be anything without someone being offended. Bullying. Cyber Bullying. Exploitation of kids, women...black lives matter, blue lives matter...shouldn't *everyone* matter?

I wish my children could have grown up like I did. In sheer, blissful ignorance. I try to shelter them. I try to shield them. No social media. No Instagram or Snap Chat. I limit their game playing. I am *all-in* as their mom, not their friend.

I don't care what everyone else is doing. I birthed them. I worked hard for it. They're mine until I deem, they are no longer babies...which may happen eventually, someday, I'm sure.

But today's world has got me missing the world I grew up in. Little things I took for granted. I remember when music was something we listened to on the radio.

You know, that antiquated thing that doesn't really exist anymore; the kind of radio that you had to walk around, holding it up...down... until you finally got the perfect clarity.

It had a metal antenna, and actual knobs that turned, only you could never figure out where on the dial you were.

On weekends, I'd listen to the weekly countdown with my tape recorder and press "record" as soon as I heard my favorite song, hoping the stupid deejay wouldn't talk over the end of it, which he always did.

And the television had just a few stations. 2, 4, 5, 7, 38 and 56.

Saturday morning cartoons were the highlight of my week, and I remember getting up early, grabbing my Cocoa Puffs and running to the sofa for a whole morning of Tom & Jerry, Scooby Doo, and the Wonder Twins! And once the channel was selected, there it stayed. No remote.

It seems everything was simpler then; easier. If you wanted to play with your friends, you went out, knocked on their door and asked them.

You didn't text or Snap...and you'd come home when the streetlights came on.

Sundays were church and family. That was it. Nothing else on a Sunday. Every Sunday we'd go to church, and then drive to my grandparents' house for a big Italian feast.

My grandmother would dance around the kitchen with her wooden spoon, and sing to my grandfather, while she stirred her sauce. He'd act like it bothered him, but then he'd wink at me and I knew he loved it just as much as I did.

While dinner was cooking, my cousins, brother and I would go exploring. We'd be gone for hours, walking along the water's edge, going to the park or the general store. We sang.

We talked and laughed. We picked flowers along the way, drank soda & ate cookies before heading back and feasting on pasta, meatballs, chicken cutlets....and two plates were never enough for my Nana. If you didn't go back for 3rds, she was insulted.

Times change. It's inevitable. I get it.

And some of the changes are better - *great* even. But there's too much noise now. Everyone has an agenda. A sense of entitlement. What happened to working hard for a life you create? No false expectations. Nobody else doing it, earning it for you.

We're all rushing it seems - rushing to the next thing. And what are we rushing to, anyway? What is so important, that we can't slow down to say hello or smile at someone passing on the street.

Are we so jaded by the news that we can't simply smile? We're on our phones, Bluetooth, or tablet...we're rushing our kids out the door, rushing our folks to downsize, rushing our lives away. Why?

Growing up, the days went by so slowly, and I felt like I'd lived a lifetime in that one, single day.

I'd spend hours laying on the grass and looking at the clouds, or running barefoot, feeling the grass beneath my feet, and tickling my toes. I'd ride my bike, I'd play kick the can or walk to the ice cream store and back, with my friends. Simple. Easy.

I'm sure these days will become my children's "good old days" too but somehow, I feel like they're missing out. Missing out on a childhood like I had. I want so desperately to recreate it for them.

So, we unplug at dinner. We sit as a family for meals. We talk. We listen. We lead through example. Provide unconditional love and support. And we pray.

And we hope the lessons we're teaching our kids will be remembered as they navigate their way in this world.

For Girls Only

So why is this book for girls only? Well, here's why. I own a little boutique in my hometown. And during prom season, I had a lot of teen girls coming into to try on prom gowns.

And as they stepped up to the mirror, I was excited. I was super silly with eagerness for them to see themselves. I was overcome with emotion...and then, I was kinda sad.

Girls, do you know what I saw? I saw their judgement. I saw their criticism. I saw it in their eyes. They looked themselves up and down. They stood on their tippy toes, held in their non-existent bellies, and sigh.

"if only I was taller..." "if only I had boobs..." "if only my arms didn't look so big..." "if only I didn't have that scar from cheer..." "if only it looked better on me than the hanger..."

Let me tell you what I saw.

I saw the beauty that comes from inside out. I saw a girl who just got accepted into the Honor Society, who's mom was so overcome with emotion, she immediately started crying - seeing you standing in that gown; nothing short of a princess.

I saw a girl who spent most of her senior year in a hospital bed, but refused to give in, to give up...and stood before the mirror, a vision. A vision of hope, of perseverance, of grace and elegance.

I didn't see flaws. I didn't see imperfections. Because there weren't any. And you know what I wanted to say to those girls?

You are perfect. You are the masterpiece that God created. You don't need to be taller, or thinner. You don't need any tweaking.

If you could see what I see, you would understand just how valuable you are. These moments are fleeting. These days will become your very best memories. You will long for them. You will reminisce with your girlfriends about them.

You won't remember the blemish. You won't remember the braces.

Who you are becoming will depend on what you tell yourself right now. RIGHT NOW. Don't fill your head with negative thoughts.

Don't listen to those voices. Silence them.

You are beautiful. You are enough. You are perfect.

Girls, listen. This time in your life can be hard. You've got challenges that we didn't have when we were your age.

You've got to deal with bullying in school and out of school – on Snap and Instagram. And even texts groups or online.

You see commercials for beauty products, weight loss, and all sorts of craziness that can completely overwhelm you. And worse yet, make you second guess yourself.

I get it. And that's why I'm writing this book right now. Consider it, more like a super-long letter from your future self.

Do you know what I mean? Like, imagine you are like, thirty years old right now. I know...roll your eyes. It's okay.

So, you're thirty and you've learned a lot over the years. And you want to sit down and write a letter to the younger version of you – things you would do differently, things you would avoid.

That's what this book is. A letter. A long, long, letter that I hope will help you avoid some of the pitfalls of pre-teen and teen years.

My hope is that this book gives you confidence, helps you realize your true worth.

And at the end of the day, I want you to look in the mirror and see a girl who can change the world.

Because you can.

Truth is, *you can do anything*. Legit. It's the truth. If you have a dream, even if it's something that like, you've never told anyone, but hold it in your heart, know that you can do it.

Here's what I know. You were not meant to be ordinary. You are here to live your best life and be your most true self.

If there's something you want in this life, you gotta believe in yourself.

You gotta believe you can have what you want, no matter what you're telling yourself and no matter what others are telling you.

And you know what I'm talking about, right? The mean girls. The stupid boys. The jerks. The kids who laugh behind your back or whisper as you walk by.

I have a secret to share with you. Those kids are just as insecure and worried about school, clothes, being popular, and all the stuff you worry about.

They just act cool and act like they're better than you because they don't want you to know they are just as lost, just as scared, just as nervous...

Yup. It's true.

Cause guess what? I was bullied by a girl in 7th grade and now she's like, my best friend.

We were in the same reading class. I sat in front of her. And my mom always, and I mean, ALWAYS put my hair in pigtails.

And every day when this girl sat behind me, she'd grab my pigtails and yank my head back.

And let me tell you something. It didn't tickle. It hurt. It hurt my hair, it hurt my head, and most importantly…it hurt my feelings.

I hated reading class. I dreaded it. I wanted to move my desk. I wanted to turn around and just punch her in that pimpled face of her.

But I didn't.

You know what I did? I didn't let her change me. I didn't let her see that it upset me. I acted as if she wasn't even there. I never turned around and yelled at her. And I definitely didn't let her see my eyes stinging with tears. I just adjusted my pigtails and carried on.

And you know what? She stopped. She realized she couldn't get to me. She realized her bullying wasn't working on me.

And now…thirty years later, we're friends. So, all the crap she put me through back in seventh grade, didn't matter. She didn't impact my life. She didn't stop me from being me. She didn't change me.

Bullies want attention. They want control. Don't give it to them. Walk away. Ignore them. When they see they can't get you mad, they'll move on. They'll stop.

So, don't let some kid – boy OR girl, stop you from becoming who you're meant to be.

If you want to try out for the baseball team, audition for the school play, or join the band. Do it!

Because guess what? When you get older, and you have responsibilities like a job, or an apartment...you will look back and regret not doing what you wanted to do.

Life goes by fast, girls – like super-fast. You have to learn to enjoy every second of it. Don't rush through it. Don't wish your birthdays away. Enjoy ten...enjoy fourteen... enjoy every single second of your age, because you only get there once. You will only be 10 once. You will only become a teen, ONCE.

Don't wish to be older so you can drive, so you can make money and buy that super cute top. You'll get there. Believe me.

"Cause the players
gonna play
And the haters gonna
hate
I'm just gonna shake
Shake it off, I shake it
off."

Taylor Swift

Social Media Addiction

I've got three kids. One is about to start his sophomore year of high school; one is going into 8th grade and my youngest is starting middle school this year – 5th grade.

They are in three different schools, with three different bus times and school starts. It's hectic to say the least.

And as my daughter is getting ready to enter 5th grade, she's worried. She's been at the same primary school since kindergarten with the same friends, the same group of teachers, and same routine.

Now that she's going to a much bigger school with students from all over the town, she's worried about being bullied or teased. She's worried that her feelings will get hurt.

She's worried she won't make any new friends. And she's worried about her friends, and if they'll be okay if she's not in the same class to protect them.

That's a lot of worry for a little girl. And it got me thinking. She can't possibly be the only one worrying about a new school year.

Looking back to when I was her age, I remember having worries too – but mine were far less critical. I worried that my mom packed my egg salad in tin foil, so it wouldn't gross out my friends at the lunch table when I opened it. I worried that she gave me grapes instead of a Devil Dog.

My worries were so small compared to those that y'all are facing right now.

That's why I'm writing this. *That's* why I want to reach out and let you know that you aren't alone in what you're feeling.

Other kids are going through it right now, just like you are.

Another thing we didn't have to worry about 'back then' was social media. It didn't exist. If we wanted to see our friends, we went out, walked down the street and knocked on their door.

With the birth of social media came the decline of personal, face to face connections.

Texting trumped phone conversations. A simple "like" became a means of staying in touch with friends and family. Impersonal. But somehow completely relevant. Completely necessary to our existence.

We have become used to instant gratification. No more watching boring t.v. commercials. You can fast forward right through them. No more missing your favorite show, you can watch it On Demand.

You don't have to write a letter with pen and paper...simply send an IM or email. Don't want to wait for the email to send and wait for them to read it? Send a text. Don't feel like typing that text? Simply send an emoji to convey what you're feeling.

Birthday parties? Who needs invitations when you can create an event on Facebook or another social media outlet? Thank you, cards,? No need to write one out. Nobody does that anymore, right?

We stay in touch with hundreds of "friends" and we convince ourselves that we really know them. We put our best selves out on social media. We crop, we filter, we fake.

***

Think about the last time you went out with your friends, whether it was the local pizza place, ice cream shop or even shopping at the mall.

What did you see when you looked around? I bet you saw a bunch of people snapping pics of their food or taking selfies. Am I right?

Hey, I'm guilty of it too. We've become addicted to it. We always keep our phones with us, we check them constantly because we might be missing a great post or snap. And Heaven forbid we lose our streaks, right?

But life goes by so fast, girls – put the phone down and look around. Take it all in. A picture can't convey the smell of a lilac bush, or the way the leaves dance to the ground when they fall in Autumn.

And a selfie is always the best image, the one you want your friends to see…or your crush. You want to look perfect, right? But what about the *real* you?

If you only take pics of the perfect you and take twenty pics to get that one perfect shot, you are missing it. You are missing everything else going on around you. Put the phone down. Enjoy the moment.

***

Recently, I had the absolute pleasure (she says sarcastically) of taking my daughter to a JoJo Siwa concert.

Six thousand screaming pre-teens in one glitterized arena. By the third song I thought for sure my ears were bleeding.

But here's what shocked me. As my daughter and I watched the concert, we saw thousands of phones raised in the air.

These kids and their moms were recording their favorite songs and looking up at their phones to make sure they were getting it – instead of actually watching the concert and enjoying being in the moment.

There's something to be said for ***not*** sharing. For keeping things to yourself. Your memories. Nobody elses.

Something to Think About: *When was the last time you didn't bring your phone with you? When was the last time you hung out with friends and just enjoyed being together? No selfies. No posts or snaps or tweets? No TikTok or YouTube watching?*

Something to Do*: Next time you head out with friends or family, take the phone if you must, but leave it in your bag, on the seat or in the car. Enjoy the time with the people in your life, in that moment. Be fully present. Ask questions. Get to know a little bit more about someone. Without the video to capture it. K?*

Body Image

When I was ten, I hung out with a bunch of the neighborhood kids. We lived within a few houses from each other, and we spent the day going from one house to the other; stopping in for snacks, drinks, or lunch.

But out of all the girls in the neighborhood, I had one best, like totally best friend. Her name was Lisa.

Lisa was super pretty with big brown eyes and long dark hair. She was tall and skinny, and all the boys had crushes on her.

I met her the day we moved into my new house, when I was just four years old. She was standing in front of her house with a bunch of other kids and moms, and I ran over to say 'hi'.

By the time I'd introduced myself and told them my whole life story, in the middle of that dead-end street, I knew we would be best friends forever.

Lisa and I lived just two houses away from each other, and if she wasn't at my house, I was at hers.

We'd share our deepest secrets; we'd talk about boys, about school, clothes, and all things girls talk about at ten years old. Sometimes we'd even get mad at each other and swear we would never be friends again.

Of course, that usually only lasted for an hour or so, and soon we were hugging and swearing we were best friends for life!

Lisa came to all my birthday parties. We used to love summers swimming in my pool, and having my dad make the absolute best ice cream sundaes.

I remember how perfect she looked in her bathing suit and I'd look at myself and the little rolls around my middle, and wish I wasn't 'fat' – I wished I was more like her. But then again, I did love Devil Dogs and all things cake.

Comparing ourselves…we are all guilty of it, right? I mean, we compare clothes and grades.

We compare our bedrooms to our friend's bedrooms – we compare pretty much everything, and we don't really even realize it, because we're so used to doing it. Right?

But listen, while I used to think I was chunky back then…when I look back, I realize that I was growing just perfectly for me. For my age. For my height. For *me*.

We all grow differently.

We all mature at different times.

Our bodies are amazing, and can be kinda scary, too.

You may have already hit puberty, or maybe you're worried that you never will because you're thirteen and still don't have boobies.

Or maybe you're ten and have already started to blossom, and you try to hide it under a heavy sweater, or wear layers in summer so people won't notice.

Girls, you're gonna get there. Don't rush it, and don't compare yourself to someone else.

And especially do not – do not read magazines or think for a single second those models haven't been touched up. Or that your favorite singer doesn't get a pimple from time to time. Or that you need to watch what you eat, so you can look like "her" – whoever "she" is.

If you haven't been living under a rock, you know about social media. You know how filters work. You know all about airbrushing a picture or changing the lighting, adding features, and all that jazz, to make a picture look better. Right?

Well, think about this. If you know how to do it, at a basic or even semi-advanced level...imagine how much greater the professionals can make someone look with all the right tools?

Magazines are designed to sell you something. To sell you a way of life, a certain look, a certain brand of makeup, perfume, or clothing. They want to make everything look perfect, so you will want whatever it is they're selling. It is not reality girls!

Those editors change everything from a certain freckle on a model's nose, to the shape of her arm. They shrink the size of their fingers, if they think they're too long, they legit change everything.

If you wanna read a magazine for the articles, go for it. But here's what I want you to do.

Step one of loving your body is to repeat after me:

"I, (your name) am beautiful, just as I am. I promise to NOT look at magazines or tv, or snap, or Instagram, or Facebook, and compare myself to someone else.

I understand that pictures can be deceiving and what I see in print or tv, may not be reality. I love myself. As is."

Say that every day if you must. Bookmark this page. Highlight it. Repeat it.

When you look back at your younger self, you will know what I'm talking about. Trust me on this.

That little ten-year old self that I thought was a little chunky? If I could go back in time, I'd dope slap that girl, and tell her she was just perfect!

What we tell ourselves matters, girls. We have to change that script from that of criticizing, to create a new script that is filled with positivity, self-love and acceptance.

You got this.

"Beauty begins the moment you decide to be yourself."

Coco Chanel

And hey, to show you that you're not alone in the body shaming/body image issues, I'll share something with you.

During the writing of this book, I was preparing to sing at my nephew's wedding. I was excited to attend because I had been asked to sing the entrance song as the bride walked down the aisle.

I had purchased my dress six months prior and couldn't wait to wear it.

And just hours before the wedding, I tried on the dress. For the FIRST time.

It didn't fit. Not even a little.

So, my go-to behavior was to start calling myself 'fat' – and shaming myself for loving all things pasta. Why do we do this, girls? **Why?**

Luckily, I have a great friend who reminded me of something I'd actually written a few weeks prior, in my blog. She texted it to me, as I was heading to the wedding, sulking at my 2nd choice outfit.

"A great friend wrote this." She had texted, along with the link. As I clicked on the link, I started to smile. I started to tear up. I needed this advice – **my own stinkin' advice**. I needed to hear it.

And while most of this won't apply to you, maybe you can share it with your mom, aunt, older sis…let her know she is beautiful as is!

"Own Who You Are"

As the owner of a women's boutique, I get to meet many different women. I've met stay-at-home moms, entrepreneurs, seamstresses, teachers and bus drivers. I've had the opportunity to talk with realtors, dentists, business professionals and caretakers. There are so many amazing women in this world. But one thing remains the same. NONE of them are happy with their body. Literally *none*. And that's what I want to correct. Today. Right now. Here.

It's not a *blatant* dislike. It's a subtle, almost unheard comment muttered while trying on a dress that is too long, too short…doesn't show the curves, shows too much curves. It's the jeans that are too tight on the hips, too loose on the hips. It's the top that accentuates the flabby part of the arm, the same top that accentuates the bony part of the arm.
My gosh ladies…I got news for you. *The clothes don't matter!* If you aren't happy with yourself, *nothing* will look right. So how do you get right with your body?
Look at it.

Your body. Right now. (*well, unless you're at work or in the middle of a meeting, in which case you shouldn't be on social media anyway!*) Go ahead…*look* at those curves. *Look* at the stretch marks, the arm waddle, the double chin…look at every inch of your *beautiful* body. Are you perfect? No. Do you have an overgrown toenail? A mole? A crooked tooth? Who knows! Who cares!

We, as women, have *got* to start loving our bodies – as we are *right in this moment.* Not what our body is *going to look like* after our diet, our new exercise program, our gallon-a-day-water-drinking-walking fad.
We have to embrace who we are with or without the added weight.

Because guess what? *Every inch of who you are is part of your history.*

I used to be a size 8. I used to have a size 7 shoe. I used to wear bikinis (*well, once on my honeymoon*). Now, I'm not a size 8. My *shoe size* is now an 8, well, truth be told, one foot is an 8, the other is still a 7. That's what happens when you have 3 babies and gain about 35 pounds during each one. Feet grow. In my case, just *one* did. I don't wear bikinis anymore and for a few years, I tried to actually avoid Summer. Yah, like — the *entire* season!

Now, I look at myself in the mirror and I see the back fat. I see a bit of flab where there used to

be muscle. I see a few wrinkles around my eyes and a forehead line that I used to hide with bangs. (*I know…I know…way to talk myself up!*)
The point is, I could spend the rest of my life on diets, on avoiding foods that I love to maintain a certain look, a certain weight. Or I could *live my life*. I could embrace who I am and the woman I've become in the process.

I'm a mom. The kind of mom who takes frequent trips to the ice cream shop with my kids because getting them one isn't as much fun as partaking in the fun of trying to eat it before it melts on a hot Summer day.

I'm a wife who enjoys going on date nights, and refuses to get a glass of water or diet *anything*, over a tasty Cosmopolitan, delicious dinner and of course, dessert of any kind – because I know these date nights are rare and I'm not going to regret a second of it!

I'm a business owner, who doesn't often find time to make a healthy lunch before I head out, or remembers to eat during a fundraiser, so I may stop on the way home and grab my favorite take out (pad thai) with dare I say, extra peanut sauce!

This is who I am now. This is me. And I have to be okay with it, or I'll spend my life trying to compare my flaws to someone else's assets. I'll spend my life hiding in a cover up, instead of hangin' with my kids in the pool. I won't go to the party because the dress makes me look fat. Guess what? It's not the dress. *I'm fat!*

Skinny girls, fat girls, tall and short girls – we all wish we were more like the other. We need to stop. We need to appreciate who we are, on the inside, and give value to *that*!

Look at yourself in a new light. Look at the woman, not the shell. See yourself as others see you. You may not even realize what others think of you. But I'll tell you this from experience: all of the women who walk through my boutique doors are incredible. Some have the weight of the world on their shoulders, but still manage to smile and offer a kind word to another…every.single.day.

Some of my customers are givers, working tirelessly to rescue animals from harm, some are nursing home helpers, feeding those who cannot feed themselves, with care and humanity. Many of my customers are teachers and work with children, literally inspiring the next generation of scientists, and freethinkers, while creating an atmosphere of hope, kindness and generosity.

And you my friend are just as magnificent. I don't care if you are a stay-at-home-mom and have Lucky Charms stuck to your floor. You are perfect.

I don't care if you are stuffing your face in the drive-thru because you are running late for pick up/drop off/meetings/appointments…You are perfect.

Everything that you have faced, dealt with, overcome…it has made you who you are.

So, stop looking at yourself in the mirror and finding fault.

And if you see someone else criticizing herself, tell *her* to stop. Let's keep building each other up. Let's keep reminding each other that we all deserve crowns.

We all deserve love – and *self-love* is the most important love of all.

Something to Think About: *How do you feel about yourself? When you look in the mirror what do you say? What do you think? Are you kind or critical?*

Something to Do: *Next time you look in the mirror, remember that (1) your body is constantly changing and to give yourself a break if you see a pimple, or have a bad hair day, (2) true beauty is not surface. True beauty is how you behave and how you treat others. Even the prettiest girl can be ugly, if she is ugly on the inside.*

Puberty

I was a late bloomer. Not only that, but I literally knew nothing about my body, outside of what I learned in those awful movies in 6th grade health class. In health class, where there were boys. And if you haven't seen "the" movie yet, saddle up ladies – you're gonna see it eventually.

So, because I knew nothing, when I finally got my period, at age, like fourteen, I thought I was dying. I literally thought something was wrong with me. No lie. I didn't tell my mom. I was horrified. I was embarrassed. And truth be told, I was *scared*. I mean, what the heck was happening?

For the first two days, I threw my underwear away. I'm gonna stop right here for a second.

Girls, I get this is *way too much* information. I get it. But I kinda wish I knew about this stuff before it happened, so I wouldn't have been freaked out or scared.

When I finally told my mom, on day three, I remember her words exactly, "My little girl is becoming a woman!" What the what? I remember thinking, "*I am no woman!*"

I was just a scared kid who was bleeding from the girl parts and not quite sure why or what it meant.

Menstruation – here's all you need to know. It's a girl thing. We all have to deal with this. You're not alone.

So, as you develop into a woman, your body will change so you can have a baby when you grow up. And part of that getting your body ready is this monthly cycle of menstruation.

But here's the most important thing girls...once you start your period, no matter what age you are - you can literally become a mama. Like, the owner of a baby. Let that sink in for a minute.

The choices you make from here on out, can stay with you forever. Be smart. Keep your body, yours. You've got the rest of your life to date, to fall in love. To have a family.

So, this period thing happens once a month. You may get cramps in your belly; you may feel a little bloated. You may be irritable. You may get a headache. Or you could be one of those girls who gets none of that and goes through it like a champ!

You'll have spotting. You'll have a little or a lot of flow. It will last 3-5 days. Maybe longer.

In the eighties, there were sanitary pads. They were about an inch thick and a foot long. When you stuck them to your underwear, it looked like you had a tail. On both ends. Not cool.

You're super lucky now because the choices are literally endless. You've got thin pads, overnights, tampons and pantiliners. So many options. None of which, make you look like you have a tail.

Another part of puberty is hair growing in places. *All the places*. And breast buds growing. And bra shopping.

And hey, don't compare yourself to your bff or your sister.

Or the girl who sits next to you in Biology. We all grow at different times, in different stages, at different ages. Okay?

There's nothing wrong with you if you're thirteen and are flat as a pancake. Be happy because once those little ladies grow, they are stuffed inside a bra and by the end of the day, you'll want to rip it off before even taking off your shoes!

Puberty – everyone deals with it. It's part of growing into the young lady you'll become. It will all be ok. I promise.

Something to Think About: *Have you been noticing changes to your body? Have you been worried that you're not growing fast enough or too fast?*

Something to Do*: This is a tough conversation starter for your mom or aunt or Grammy to have with you. It might be awkward. More for them, I'm sure. But maybe you'll want to show them this section and start a conversation with them. It's a natural progression in growing up. And they are there to help you navigate through it. Trust them.*

Teen Dating & Violence

This is a hard one. Even as I'm typing, I'm worried about the words I'm going to use, the way I'm going to tell you some of the things I had to learn the hard way – things I want to spare you from ever having to deal with.

Okay, here goes. I grew up in the 70s. (Don't do the math, k? I'm 51 years old as I write this.) My pre-teen and teen years were filled with crushes and school dances. My friends and I always went to the dances as a group, getting ready together in one of our bedrooms, spraying way too much *Love's Baby Soft,* and hoping the cute boy would ask us to dance.

We were so innocent. We were so sheltered. I didn't know how to kiss.

I didn't know anything about anything boy-related. And I didn't care.

Well, not until I was thirteen years old, and I was asked to dance by a total cutie, while spending a week during the summer at my cousin's house.

As we danced, he leaned down and kissed me. It was wet. It was awkward. I was horrified. I mean, I didn't even know him!

After the dance ended, he asked for my number and I got his. I remember coming home and telling my parents all about him and being nervous about what I'd actually say to him over the phone; the corded phone, girls – the one that only went about two feet without being pulled from the wall. The wall, that the phone was attached to!

There was no hiding in my room to chat. There we were, my mom and dad and me, waiting for the phone to ring.

Waiting to hear from Jimmy.

***

Fast forward a few years. I'm now fifteen. The long distance "dating" between Jimmy and I didn't last very long. I mean, it's hard to date when your dad has to drive you to the date, because neither of you are old enough to drive.

So, I'm a sophomore in high school, dating who would end up being my first love. My high school sweetheart.

We'd hold hands in the hallway. He'd walk me home and we'd listen to records (yes, actual records) on the stereo. If we wanted to hear the song again, or change the song, we had to get off the sofa, pick up the needle and move it to the next groove. Times were hard, girls.

We went to movies and out for ice cream.

He came to my house to pick me up, spent time talking with my parents, and never once, beeped the horn to have me run out to him. He was respectful. He was a gentleman.

After dating for a few years, we got engaged one snowy Christmas Eve. I soon realized however, that I was simply too young to settle down, and we parted the best of friends.

***

As innocent as those first two experiences were, things changed as I got a few years older. Nineteen. The year that changed the course of the rest of my life.

Dave was a college guy. He was smart. He came from a family of lawyers and doctors. He was handsome, he was funny. And he was horribly abusive.

Not at first. And not for a while. It happened so gradually; I didn't recognize it as abuse.

And that's why I'm letting you know right now. At your age right now. Whether you're twelve or fifteen, or even as young as nine. You need to know *now*, before you really start dating, so you can spot the difference between genuine concern and sheer control.

When someone cares about you, he won't be jealous. He won't get mad if you talk to someone in school, other than him. I used to think jealousy was a sign of love. I used to think if he was jealous, it meant that he must really care. NO. That is not true.

If he is jealous, it is because he is insecure. It has *nothing* to do with love. And it has nothing to do with you - at all.

Another thing I noticed too late, was his controlling behavior. I used to have a lot of friends in high school. I was also super close to my family.

Over time, he demanded more time with me, and would get upset if I was late calling or seeing him. He'd question where I was, who I was with, and if I even cared about him anymore. Controlling behavior is not love.

Blaming. Threatening...it's all part of abuse girls. Telling you "You made me mad." Or "If you didn't do X, I wouldn't be angry. This is your fault." Making you feel stupid or inferior. Or worse yet, calling you names and making you feel like you deserve it. None of that is okay.

In your preteen and teen years, you are still learning about yourself. You are still trying to figure it all out.

Give yourself time. Don't rush into dating because your friend is, or you feel pressured to do so.

And should you start dating, remember, nobody has the right to make you feel small. Nobody has the right to try and control you, disrespect or ridicule you.

And girls, while we're talking about teen dating and violence, know this; a push or shove is never okay. A boy should never, and I mean NEVER hit a girl. That is abuse. That is not okay.

It has nothing to do with what you were wearing, what you said, who you were talking to. It has nothing to do with you at all. It is abuse. End of story.

Remember who the heck you are. Adjust your crown and carry on.

I got wrapped up in a very abusive relationship because I was too naïve to realize what was happening. I didn't know the signs. I didn't realize jealousy and control weren't signs of love, but abuse.

And I almost lost my life as a result of it. But I survived. And I survived with a purpose of exposing those who lurk in the darkness – to hurt and destroy.

The bullies, the abusers, and yes, even the problems that you're facing or about to face in these teen years: Peer pressure, drug and alcohol use, vaping, depression.

There's a lot of pressure on y'all that I just didn't have to deal with. And as a mom of three, I am in a constant state of controlled panic.

But you know what? I know you totally got this. You are smart girls. You are brave and you are fierce.

My ten-year-old daughter reminds me daily. She defends others and *herself*. She's tough and tender. She is smart and sassy.

But sometimes she does need a hug. We all do. Right now, this is my hug to you. Whether you need it or not.

Something to Think About: *What are some of the things you like about yourself. Are you smart, are you funny? Do you care about people? Stop others from bullying? Volunteer? What makes you special?*

Something to Do*: Create a list of all your best traits and tape them to your mirror. And at the bottom of that list, I want you to write, "Nobody is worth taking all of this away from me!" "Nobody is gonna change the best parts of me!"*

"You may encounter many defeats, but you must not be defeated. In fact, it may be necessary to encounter the defeats, so you can know who you are, what you can rise from, how you can still come out of it."

Maya Angelou

Bullying

So, we touched on this earlier with my story about the girl in seventh grade who pulled my hair. But today, bullying is more than just pulling someone's pigtails.

Today, you're dealing with bullying in schools, on the bus, and on social media platforms.

What is bullying, anyway? Let's be clear, girls. Bullying is a serious issue, and if you're being bullied, you need to let someone know; a teacher, a parent, a trusted adult. Make it known. Don't keep it a secret or try to deal with it on your own.

A bully, by definition:

verb
gerund or present participle: **bullying**

1. seek to harm, intimidate, or coerce (someone perceived as vulnerable).
"her 11- year-old son has been constantly bullied at school"

Bullying is no joke. It is antagonistic behavior. It is a repeated behavior. It is unwanted. And it has lasting problems for the kids being bullied.

Kids who bully want control – much like my abusive boyfriend when I was nineteen. Bullying can be done with physical strength or by gaining access to some type of embarrassing information on you and using it to hurt you.

For example; using a pic that you've posted or sent to someone in private, and them gaining access to it, and sharing it with everyone they know.

Girls, that's why it's *so important* to watch what you send via text, snap or Instagram. Anything you send from a pic to a text can be screenshot and used to publicly embarrass you.

And there are other kinds of bullying to look out for: threats, spreading rumors, attacking someone physically or verbally, and even by excluding someone from a group on purpose.

Okay, so because this is such an important topic, I did a little research. The following was taken directly from the www.stopbullying.gov website, and is a great resource if you are dealing with a bully. Here's what you need to know:

There are three types of bullying:

- **Verbal bullying** is saying or writing mean things. Verbal bullying includes:
  - Teasing
  - Name-calling
  - Inappropriate sexual comments
  - Taunting
  - Threatening to cause harm

- **Social bullying,** sometimes referred to as relational bullying, involves hurting someone's reputation or relationships. Social bullying includes:

- Leaving someone out on purpose
- Telling other children not to be friends with someone
- Spreading rumors about someone
- Embarrassing someone in public

- **Physical bullying** involves hurting a person's body or possessions. Physical bullying includes:
    - Hitting/kicking/pinching
    - Spitting
    - Tripping/pushing
    - Taking or breaking someone's things
    - Making mean or rude hand gestures

Bullying can occur during or after school hours. While most reported bullying happens in the school building, a significant percentage also happens in places like on the playground or the bus. It can also happen travelling to or from school, or on the Internet.

Something to Think About: *Have you ever been a victim of bullying? Have you known someone that has? What did you do about it? What could you have done differently?*

Something to Do: *Talk to a member of the school faculty, a guidance counselor, a principal – and find out what the policy is on bullying. Read it.*

Girls, you can *make a difference. One voice can change history. Perhaps join the Student Council or create a Pro-Inclusion/Anti-Bullying group. And if you see something, say something.*

"I know and I speak from experience, that even in the midst of darkness, it is possible to create light and share warmth with one another..."

Elie Wiesel

The Mean Girl

As I was writing the section on bullying, it occurred to me – what if *you*, reading this right now – what if *you're* the bully? What if *you're* the mean girl?

What if you're the one who makes fun of someone, gossips behind someone's back or makes them cry on the bus? What if you're the one who group texts everyone and shares a secret that you know you weren't supposed to share? What if?

Here's all I wanna say. As a girl who was bullied, as a mom of a girl who was bullied, **please stop**.

That's it. Just stop. I'm not going to shame you. I'm not going to ask why you do it. I already know.

This is a hard time to be a kid. There are all sorts of things going on that we didn't have to worry about. I feel like our world was smaller, safer and all-around easier.

We are bombarded with bad news on the television, in the news and on social media. Everything that happens, happens in real-time and we know about it instantly.

And there are pressures now that we didn't have years ago.

I mean, preschoolers are expected to read at a college level now! Well, maybe not at a college level, but expectations have definitely grown since I was a kid.

And growing up we had like, two pairs of shoes; one for dress and sneakers. And every year, during the last week in August, we'd pile in the car, and head to Sears Roebuck Department store for back-to-school shoes.

And we weren't the only ones. Everyone. Like, every kid in school would go with their moms, during the last week of August. We were all getting our new shoes. One pair. And we were excited and super grateful for that one pair of shoes.

Now there is so much pressure to have the best, to wear the best – we are inundated with commercials; celebrities telling us how to dress, how to act, what to wear.

Celebrities telling us what our political views should be. It's all too much. It's all **too…much**!

Now let's be clear, I'm not excusing bad behavior. Every day *you* have a choice. Actually, many choices.

Whatever is causing you to be the bully, to be the mean girl…know this. You can change right now. Today.

Hear what I'm saying. It is totally doable to change bad behavior!

Listen, I get it. Parents sometimes divorce. Loved ones pass away. Bad things happen. Maybe you had to move away from friends or leave the only home you've ever known.

Maybe you tried out for the basketball team, and someone else got the last spot on the team.

Whatever has happened so far in your life, whatever has caused you pain and heartbreak, you gotta let it go. Not because it's the right thing to do – although that is a part of healing…no, you gotta let it go because if you hold onto anger, it changes the core of who you are, of who you'll become.

Okay, so lots of bad stuff has been going on, but here's the great news – you have the power to change. Right now. You have control over your own feelings.

You don't need to be the mean girl. Instead, be the girl that helps another find her worth. Be the girl who sits with the new kid, in the lunchroom. Be the girl who compliments, who finds joy in the small things, who is grateful, who is kind.

Be THAT girl.

Because we are really all the same. We are all trying to find our way in this world. We are all struggling with something.

All of us have *something*. So why not try and help someone else get through *their* something. In the end, they may help you with yours.

And that's how friendships form and grow.

It's never too late. Choose today. Choose now. *Right now*. If you need to make it right with someone, make it right. And not by text. Not snap. In person. Face to face. Eye to eye.

Be the change. The world really needs a superhero right now.

Something to Think About: *How have your actions and words hurt someone else? A sibling? A friend? What would happen if you used your words to heal? What would that look like to you?*

Something to Do*: For the next three weeks, be the hero. When you do something consistently for three weeks, it becomes a habit. What new habits can you create? How can you become a hero in your family? Your community? Your school or neighborhood?*

"Do not look for
healing
at the feet of those
who broke you."

Rupi Kaur

Depression & Suicide

There is no easy way to have this conversation. There is no way for me to write it out – as if there was some sort of manual for being happy and carefree for the rest of your life. That's not life. And it's not reality.

The reality is, this age is hard. H-A-R-D hard. I'll go one further...*every* age is hard. **Until it isn't**. What do I mean by that?

Well, you may not remember this, but when you were a baby, you couldn't talk. You struggled to communicate. You pounded your fists; you banged your head against hard surfaces. You tried to communicate. Eventually, you learned to talk. Ahhh...it was so much easier, right?

Then, as a toddler, you couldn't walk. *Super* frustrating.

You scooted around on your bum, or, if you were like my oldest, you got from place to place by sliding your head around like a mop.

Eventually, you got the hang of it. Am I right?

As you grew, the level of difficulties got harder. You attended preschool or kindergarten. You had to make new friends. That was hard, right? Learning…learning anything. Hard. Until you understood it. Until it became easier.

And now, now you're in the thick of it. You are in what everyone recalls in their adulthood as, "the hardest times ever!"- which of course, is being a kid in middle or high school.

Why the heck is it so hard, anyway? I'll tell you why. The first 81 pages of this book. And the next 30!

Y'all have a lot on your plate. Kids are mean. Awkward. Unsure. Insecure. We haven't quite figured out who we are yet, and sometimes we look to others, maybe we look to the "cool kids" for validation. And if we don't get it, it hurts.

And we keep it in, don't we? We hold those feelings in because we don't want our folks, our grandparents, our friends, our foster families...we won't want anyone to know that we're hurting.

But guess what? Remember how I said every age is hard until it isn't? Just as you had to struggle earlier in life to walk, to talk, to make friends, to learn...you did it! You got through it.

Whatever you're going through right now, is temporary. Listen...it's **TEMPORARY**. It will not last. I can guarantee you it will not last.

You might be dealing with a bully. You might be struggling at home; you might be struggling with grades. You might feel alone. Isolated. You might feel like the only answer is to check out. Be gone. End the pain. End the hurt.

But know this – whatever…**WHATEVER you are dealing with is not MORE IMPORTANT than YOU.**

Read that again. I'll wait.

Whatever you are dealing with, there is a solution. There is an answer. There is hope.

You might not think so, but as a survivor of domestic abuse, I am here to tell you, there *IS* light at the end of whatever dark tunnel you're in right now.

At 22 years old, I didn't think I'd live to see another birthday. I was broken.

I was bruised. I was incredibly sad. And there was a minute...a split second, that I didn't think I could go on.

But I stood up, brushed the hair from my eyes, wiped away my tears, and looked at myself in the mirror. And decided I would NOT become a statistic.

And I reached out. I asked for help. I slowly became stronger. My self-esteem and self-confidence came back. I finished my college classes and got my degree. I went on to speak at Domestic Violence Awareness benefits.

I married. Had three children and live my best life every day.

Girls, whatever you're going through...

It's temporary.

Do not let it have power over you.

Not to get all statistic-y or anything, but check this out:

*Statistics on Teenage Depression and Suicide**

1. Suicide is the third leading cause of death for the 12-18 age demographic. When the age demographic is expanded to 10-24, suicide becomes the second leading cause of death.

2. Studies show that at least 90% of teens who kill themselves have some type of mental health problem.

3. The number of teens who thought about killing themselves at the time of their worst or most recent episode of major depressive disorder: 1.8 million.

4. States in the US spend nearly $1 billion annually on medical costs associated with completed suicides and suicide attempts by youth up to 20 years of age.

5. 14%. That's the percentage of teens who suffered at least one episode of depression within the last 12 months.

6. More teens die from suicide than from cancer, heart disease, AIDS, birth defects, stroke, pneumonia, influenza, and chronic lung disease combined.

7. The number of suicide attempts that are estimated to happen in the United States every day by teens: 5,400.

8. 4 of 5 teens who attempt suicide have given clear warning signs as to their intentions.

9. About 11% of adolescents have an ongoing depressive disorder by age 18.

10. Depressed teens with coexisting disorders such as substance abuse problems are less likely to respond to treatment for depression.

11. The issue that teens face with treatment for depression is that many anti-depressants also have a side effect that may contribute to an increased level of suicidal thoughts.

12. The top 3 methods used in suicides of young people include firearms [45%], suffocation [40%], and poisoning [8%].

13. Of the reported suicides in the 10 to 24 age group, 81% of the deaths were males and 19% were females.

14. Girls are more likely to report failed suicide attempts than boys.

15. Native American/Alaskan Native/First Nations youth have the highest rates of suicide-related fatalities.

16. Hispanic teens are more likely to report suicide attempts than any other racial or ethnic demographics.

17. 16% of high school students have reported that they have seriously contemplated committing suicide.

18. Teens who self-identify with the LGBTQI demographic are have suicide risks that are 4x higher than the general teen population.

19. Only 13% of teens actually create a plan for their suicide before they actually attempt one.

20. 157,000. That's the number of teens who receive medical care every year because of self-inflicted injuries

*taken from www.healthresourcefunding.org

Depression is common. It is not something to be ashamed of. It is not something you can just brush off. Your feelings matter.

Suicide is temporary. Unnecessary. Not okay. You are worthy. You are loved. You are important. And if you don't think so, call me, and I'll tell you just how valued you are.

Something to Think About: *Do you ever feel sad and you have no idea why? Just sort of overall sad and numb? Do you feel like your problems are weighing heavy on your mind? Or, do you have a friend or know someone who seems depressed?*

Something to Do*: Don't keep this to yourself. Be strong and tell someone. A guidance counselor at school, a trusted friend or adult, mom, dad, grandparents…someone. You are not alone. We all go through stuff at different times in our lives, but it is temporary. It will not last.*

Smokin' & Drinkin'

I'm typing this with fingers crossed. I'm hoping y'all are smart enough, secure enough and fierce enough to know better than to ever begin any of those things. But with teen years, comes peer pressure, experimenting and being kinda stupid.

So, the purpose of this chapter is to have a real conversation about it. And in keeping with being true to yourself, I want you to learn the facts before you're ever confronted with making the decision to 'try it.'

Here are some facts: Smoking is probably worse for you than you think. For example, 438,000 Americans die from smoking-related diseases annually.

More Facts – I took these directly from the American Lung Association:

Cigarette smoke contains over 4,800 chemicals, 69 of which are known to cause cancer.

Smoking is directly responsible for approximately 90 percent of lung cancer.

Each day, nearly 6,000 children under 18 years of age start smoking; of these, nearly 2,000 will become regular smokers. That is almost 800,000 annually.

Approximately 90 percent of smokers begin smoking before the age of 21.

If current tobacco use patterns persist, an estimated 6.4 million children will die prematurely from a smoking-related disease. Tobacco use in kids your age are associated with a range of heath-compromising behaviors.

Some of those behaviors include being involved in fights, carrying weapons, engaging in high-risk sexual behavior and using alcohol and other drugs.

Okay, lots of information there, and not fun to read, I'm sure.

Growing up, I used to see commercials for smoking. The ladies always looked so sophisticated, and the guys were all crazy handsome!

Smoking was considered 'cool' – but my mom told me not to smoke, and I didn't. Back then, we listened to our parents and did what they said, out of respect (and fear of a firm slap on the butt).

But again, times are different now.

And while society has come a long way, banning cigarette commercials and taking cigarettes off convenient store shelves, teens are still drawn to the 'cool' aspect of it.

Often succumb to peer pressure. And don't even get me started on teen drinking!

"Alcohol is the most widely used substance among America's teens and young adults, posing substantial health and safety risks. Believe it or not, the average age for a first drink is 14." *

So, what's a girl to do to avoid under-age drinking? Keep yourself busy with activities that are not conducive to alcohol consumption, such as sports, clubs, or other recreational events.

Here are some great ideas: *

- Use your parents as an excuse; for example, tell your friends that they will smell the alcohol or explain the ways you will get in trouble if you get caught.

- Establish and maintain healthy relationships with other peers who don't drink and won't pressure you to do so.

- Be aware that people often "talk themselves up" and that they likely aren't drinking as much as they say they are. Be aware that social perceptions are often skewed.

- If you do find yourself at a party where there is drinking, ask for soda or fruit juice so you are drinking something. Others may be less likely to pressure you if they see you with a drink, even if it doesn't actually contain alcohol.

- Develop a plan for handling peer pressure when it arises. Think of things you can say ahead of time when offered alcohol so you won't be caught off guard.

- Talk with your parents about drinking and how to handle difficult situations.

- Understand the risks and potential dangers of underage drinking and make a decision to stay sober and hang out with others who will do the same.

Girls let's be real here. The United States is dealing with an epidemic; drug overdoses are literally killing you.

According to teen drug overdose statistics, the number of teen drug users that are doing drugs and fall victim to accidental overdosing when doing drugs.

The teen drug overdose statistics show the 15-24 age group is at the highest risk for overdosing among teens and young adults.

What may start out as a dare, to try a cigarette, or to impress someone, could turn into an addiction, and a progression to marijuana or something far worse. Cocaine, heroin, meth.

The best way to rid the United States of this epidemic is to never start. Never pick up a cigarette. Hang with friends who are like-minded and smart, who have goals for their future.

So, what happens if you are doing all the right things, hangin' with kids who aren't into smoking and drinking, but then something happens.

One day you're hangin' out with your bestie, and she lights up a cigarette, joint, or starts vaping. She tells you its no big deal. She heard from a friend on Snap Chat that it will relax her, because you know...she had a really stressful week with school, not making the cheer team, her dog died...

She tells you to try it. She doesn't want to do it alone. And c'mon, you're best friends. It's no big deal. *What are you gonna do?*

Here's what I want you to know right now. A friend, a real friend, will not pressure you or guilt you into doing something that you *know* is wrong. And if you say 'no' – a true friend will not keep harping on you to try it, just to make themselves feel better about what they are about to do.

It will not be easy to walk away, in this moment, I know. I get it. Peer pressure is hard. And being pressured by a "friend" can be confusing. If you say 'no' will you still be friends? If you say 'yes' what happens to your body? Your brain?

Kids are vaping and ending up in comas, with collapsed lungs, or worse…death. Is your need for friends bigger than your need for life? Is your love of your friend bigger than your love of self?

I urge you to choose YOU. Saying 'no' isn't easy. But if you lose a friend over it, was she really a friend at all?

The future is literally yours. And the choices you make today, will impact your life, for better or worse.

Something to Think About: *What would you do if someone offered you a cigarette or asked you to vape in the girl's bathroom? What if someone handed you a drink during a sleepover or while hanging out at a friend's house?*

Something to Do*: Plan your answer in advance, so you won't be taken off-guard if this situation arises. Remember, friends – real friends, won't pressure you or ask you to do something you aren't comfortable with.*

* Partnership for Drug-Free Kids website.

School & Time-Management Stress

Let me ask you. Are you totally stressed? Are you finding that there's just not enough time in the day to get done everything you need to get done?

Stress increases at school and the older you get, the more projects need to get finished, more testing, and cap stone projects (whatever the heck those are!)

Stress to get good grades, stress over bad grades, stress over missing homework or in class assignments, due to sickness.

I mean, gosh, you miss a few days of school and you go from an A- to a C-.

Toss into the mix sports and extracurricular activities – eating dinner in the car between flag football, dance and theater.

Now add in finding time to hang out with friends and being increasingly distracted by social media. Your phone is literally always with you. It's in your pocket, on your desk, in your backpack. You're getting texts from teachers, from friends, from your folks.

How y'all learn to juggle all of these expectations is beyond me and I'm sure creates a great amount of stress.

You're expected to act like an adult. You're expected to handle things independently and follow through on the right decisions.

As you get a bit older, get a job, take drivers ed classes, and manage your finances.

It's no wonder your rooms are a mess! When do you have time to clean them? When do you have time for anything?

There's too much on your shoulders, and sometimes it's because you really want to take guitar, dance and drama. Sometimes its because you want to be a part of the Student Council, the Cheer squad, the whatever...

But as a former teen, I got news for you. It goes by super-fast. Like, in the blink of an eye you're 18, then 20...then working and paying rent. Being an adult. For the rest of your life. The **rest-of-your-life**.

Don't overdo it. Don't overschedule yourself.

Don't wake up worried that you have a dozen things to get done in a single day and stress over how you're going to get it all done.

When I was a new mom, I worried that I wasn't doing enough for my son. I signed him up for a local 'movement' class with parachutes, and slides. And you know what? My son hated it.

And I hated rushing around to get there by the class start time, because if you missed the first few minutes, you had to wait until the instructor let you in the play area.

As he got older, I signed him up for soccer – hated it. Karate…lasted to Advanced Blue belt and quit when he broke his arm. There was flag football, tee ball, baseball. There was Webelo's and Boy Scouts.

One afternoon, on the way home from yet another soccer game, I looked in the rear-view mirror. My son had fallen asleep. And I'd realized. He was exhausted. It was too much. Too much running around. Too much in the car back and forth.

So, we stopped. Everything. Goodbye karate. Goodbye soccer. Goodbye flag football.

I stopped overscheduling my kids and as they grew older and could decide for themselves what they were truly passionate about, we chose that.

My oldest now plays baseball and is just a few ranks away from Eagle Scout. During the school year, he takes guitar lessons for thirty minutes a week.

My middle also takes guitar lessons once a week for thirty-minutes and plays baseball seasonally.

He too, is a Scout. They are together in most of their hobbies and passions. They are not overscheduled.

My youngest has tried theater, tap and ballet. It's not her thing. She's not into gymnastics or athletics. And that's totally fine with me.

The way I look at it, y'all are only this age ONCE. You will have plenty of time to overschedule yourselves with work, and family and kids and responsibilities. Someday.

Enjoy being a kid. If you don't want to take piano lessons, don't. If you aren't excited about basketball, so be it.

Be a kid. Go outside and play. Take off your shoes and socks and feel the grass between your toes.

Take time to enjoy life. Take time to enjoy *this time in your life*. You are only this age once.

Don't stress yourself out overscheduled. And if you feel like you are stressed, talk to your adult person – a mom, dad, a stepparent, aunt or uncle, teacher or guidance counselor. Talk to *someone* and tell them how you're feeling.

Your feelings matter. You matter. Never forget that.

Something to Think About: *Are you overscheduled? Do you feel like there's not enough time in the day to get things done?*

Something to Do: *Make a list of all your extracurricular activities. Now rewrite them in order of importance to you? Which can you take away? Which can you keep doing without negatively impacting your schoolwork?*

"You are braver than you believe, and stronger than you seem, and smarter than you think."

Christopher Robin

Just Like You

Remember in the beginning of this book I told you that I'm not famous? Well, I wanted you to know that there have been actual famous people who went through some stuff. Hard stuff. Stuff like maybe you're going through. Or might go through.

I bet you even know some of these people. People you've had to do a school report on, ***amiright?***

Here's the list. Take a minute. I bet you'll see some familiar names; names of people you thought had it made, had things handed to them, or that perhaps success came easy to them.

Helen Keller: Helen Keller is famous for overcoming the misfortune of being both deaf and blind to become a leading humanitarian of the 20th century.

Can you even imagine how difficult the easiest of tasks was for her? Can you imagine how frustrated she was? Her obstacles were plenty, but she overcame. She survived. She thrived. She made history.

Jim Carrey: Carrey is known for his talent, his funny faces, his personality that seems to burst onto the movie screen as a talented comedian. It's hard to believe that as a child he was seriously depressed.

Depression is immobilizing. It's debilitating. But somehow, he overcame that depression, turned the funny faces he used to make his mom feel better (she was very sick) into a career that spans decades.

F. D. Roosevelt: Franklin D. Roosevelt was the only American president who served more than two terms (1933-1945), became extremely sick, which resulted in a permanent paralysis.

Because he was concerned with his public image, he refused to be seen in a wheelchair and made great efforts to stand upright while giving speeches.

Agatha Christie: Okay, if you're a book lover like myself, you've read one of her books. She is world renowned. But did you know that she used to be dyslexic as a young child?

This disorder might have stopped Agatha from writing her books, but her strength and ambition helped her to overcome this problem and to become one of the most famous people in the world. Think about that. Dyslexia. And you're a writer. Can you imagine how difficult that must have been for her to overcome? Was it worth it? Absolutely.

Okay, this next one is amazing. I'd personally never known of this man until researching this book.

Aron Lee Ralston: He became famous after having been in a horrific accident. Aron was an experienced mountain climber and while hiking in Utah, his hand was crushed by a boulder, and the boulder pinned it against the canyon's wall. There he stayed for 5 days, trying to free himself. To survive, he amputated his arm with a knife. Then, he climbed back and was found by rescuers in time to save his life. Still climbs and his disability does not stop him from doing what he loves.

That's hard-core, girls. Tell you what, the next time you decide to have yourself a pity party, I want you to think of this guy! This guy knows how to overcome an obstacle. He cut off his arm to survive!

Joan of Arc (1412-1431): Joan was a 14-year-old illiterate peasant girl. However, despite the prejudice against both peasants and women, she persuaded the Dauphin of France to lay siege to the town of Orleans. She correctly prophesied the Dauphin would be again crowned King of France. Seven years after her death, the French had defeated the English. *

J.K. Rowling: Rowling became the world's best-selling children's author, despite managing on benefits as a single mother. Initially, her manuscript for Harry Potter was rejected by several publishers. Harry freakin' Potter! One of the best-selling book series of our time.

Stephen Hawking: Despite suffering from motor neurone disease, Hawking has helped popularise scientific concepts and make ground-breaking discoveries. Stephen Hawking passed away, March 2018.

Thomas Edison: C'mon, you knew he'd be on this list! Thomas Edison was fired from his job, when a chemical experiment, leaked acid on to his boss' desk. However, despite being almost penniless, Edison rose to be the most prolific inventor of his generation.

Walt Disney: The man behind the happiest place on earth was fired by the editor of a newspaper because he "lacked imagination and had no good ideas." He then started several businesses that failed and ended with bankruptcy.

That didn't stop him from bringing life to one of the most beloved animated characters, Mickey Mouse and becoming the recipient of 22 academy awards. And um, hello? Walt Disney World?

*Citation: **Pettinger, Tejvan**. "PEOPLE WHO OVERCAME DIFFICULT ODDS", Oxford, www.biographyonline.net, 11th Feb 2013. Last updated 1 March 2018.

A Letter from Me

Girls, if I could talk to you in person, I would sit you down, probably at a cute little cafe, look you in the eye, and tell you that you're worth it. Listen to me.

You are worth it!

Everything that has brought you to this point in life right now, it has shaped you. Some for the better. Some for the worse. But it is who you are. You matter.

Life is a challenge. But it is also a gift. It can be amazing or downright awful, and how it is, depends on how you see it. You don't need to have what everyone else has. You don't have to be something you're not to fit in. You don't need to act a certain way.

Because "you" are perfect. With all your blemishes, scrapes and scratches that life has presented...you are becoming the best version of you. Experiences mold you.

They teach you what you want, and what you don't want. They teach you what you are willing to tolerate, and what you absolutely will not accept. It's a process. It takes time.

The girl I was at 16, and 21, and 34, and 40...is not who I am now. Every year, I become a better version of myself, because I *choose* to. I could stay content with my life and my goals.

I could look at everything that's happened in my life and feel bad for myself. I could stay in a rut. I could sit back and just be. But what if I try to become more?

It's easy to do what everyone else is doing.

It's safe. But to stand on your own, takes a certain level of crazy. A certain level of confidence. Yes, it's terrifying.

But every stage of your life will teach you something. I learned that I'm an over-achiever, a survivor, a wife, a mother, an entrepreneur, a friend. I learned that love is fleeting. Hold on to it when you find it.

I'm learning still – learning to say 'no,' to sometimes be a little selfish, to take a break when I need one. I'm learning that love has highs and lows, but it is so worth every minute.

I'm learning balance. I'm learning to eat healthier, despite my love of cake. I'm learning. And so are you.

Who you are right now is not who you are going to become. Give yourself a break!

I know. You're reading this and you're like, "Um hello, you don't even know me." And you're right. I don't. But I do know this. You were born for a reason. You are here for a reason.

Don't waste your time on this earth comparing yourself to others. When you compare yourself to someone else, you are neglecting to realize all they've overcome to get to where they are.

You've skipped the process. You've fast forwarded to where they are now and comparing yourself to something you have no business comparing yourself to.

When you compare yourself to others, you are comparing their strengths to your weaknesses. You're comparing the beginning of your story, to the middle of theirs. Does that make sense?

You do you.

Every day wake up and try to be a better version of yourself.

Every day try to make a difference; in your own life, in the life of those around you, in this world.

Believe it or not, one voice does make a difference. One kind deed can start a ripple effect. It just takes one.

Truth be told, you're *already* pretty great. Never forget that.

You. You're great! You are. Not your bff, your frenemy. Not the girl who can do a perfect handstand, or the one who aces every test.

Stop comparing yourself.

"A flower doesn't worry about competing with the flower next to it. It just blooms."

Isn't that crazy amazing? Read it again. Out loud. To a friend. To your mom. To your sister. To another fierce and brilliant chic like yourself.

A flower doesn't worry about competing with the flower next to it. It just blooms.

I'm guilty of it too. I used to compare myself to others, instead of just accepting that we all get to wear the crown. We all get to bloom, in our own time.

Did I make my point absolutely clear? Stop comparing. Seriously, stop it.

And while I'm at it, I'll tell you this: don't give up. Don't give in to those to criticize you, or maybe don't understand you. That's on them.

Don't second guess yourself. Don't let your dreams die because you're afraid.

Find the beauty in every single day. Find a reason to be grateful. Find a cause you can get behind. Find someone that makes you want to be a better you.

Don't judge. *You do you*. Let them do them. And every once in a while, eat cake.

Conclusion

Girls, listen. They'll tell you, you can't. *Don't listen to them.*

They'll tell you, you aren't smart enough. You aren't good enough. *Don't listen to them.*

They'll say you're not talented enough. You're too clumsy. You won't make the team. You can't sing. You won't get cast in the musical. You're not smart enough for chess club. *Don't listen to them.*

They'll shatter your dreams, wreck your confidence, break your spirit. *Don't listen to them.*

They will try to poke holes in the goals you're trying to achieve. If given the chance, they'll keep you *exactly* where you are – scared to try.

Scared to be more than you thought possible. You want more. You have passion, a desire, a dream, a grand plan for the future.

If you listen to them, they will break you completely. They will make you give up. They will keep you in the status quo. They will ruin your chance for the future you're trying to create.

These aren't your friends. These aren't your parents, your teacher or karate instructor. These aren't the words of your enemy.

These are far worse.
These are *your* words.
These are *your* thoughts.
These are the words you tell *yourself.*

But I'm here to tell you, you *can*. Imagine if you re-trained your thoughts. Imagine if everything you've ever wanted was *entirely possible*, and you believed in yourself? Can you imagine it?

Words are powerful. Yes, words from those we admire, respect and cherish...those words matter. But what we tell *ourselves* can be crippling. Don't listen to those words of defeat, of negativity.

You want to start your own YouTube Channel? *Do it.*

You want to try out for cheer, dance or acting? *Do it.*

You want to join the boxing team? Try your hand at basketball? Computer Club? *Do it!*

You want to live in the suburbs with a husband, three kids, five chickens, a dog, and some goldfish? *Have at it! Oh wait, that's me.*

You can have anything you've ever wanted. You *can*.

And when you tell yourself, "You've got this, girl!" ***Listen.***

"Kids go where there is excitement. They stay where there is love."

Zig Ziglar

Other Books by Dolly Hardy
Available on Amazon & Kindle Edition

Means of Escape
The Last Dance
Actually, I Can (and so can you)

Follow Dolly on Instagram @shopgirldolly

or her blog at www.according2dolly.com

Check out her boutique
Dolly's Boutique – Simple Treasures
819 Broad Street
Weymouth, MA 02189
www.facebook.com/shopgirldolly
www.dollys.boutique

About the Author

Dolly Hardy is a graduate of UMASS Boston, and the owner of Dolly's Boutique in Weymouth, Massachusetts, where she lives with her husband, Shawn and three children. Her first book, Means of Escape, is her true survival story of domestic abuse.

Made in the USA
Monee, IL
09 February 2020

21396293R00069